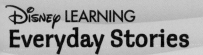

Disney LEARNING
Everyday Stories

DISNEY · PIXAR
INSIDE OUT
Hotheads

Written by Sheila Higginson • Illustrated by the Disney Storybook Artists
Special thanks to Dr. Renée Cherow-O'Leary

Lerner Publications ◆ Minneapolis

Lerner Publications Company
A division of Lerner Publishing Group, Inc.
241 First Avenue North
Minneapolis, MN 55401 USA

For reading levels and more information, look up this title at
www.lernerbooks.com.

Library of Congress Cataloging-in-Publication Data

The Cataloging-in-Publication Data for *Hotheads: An* Inside Out *Story*
is on file at the Library of Congress.
ISBN 978-1-5415-3250-2 (lib. bdg.)
ISBN 978-1-5415-3288-5 (pbk.)
ISBN 978-1-5415-3252-6 (eb pdf)

LC record available at https://lccn.loc.gov/2017050937

Manufactured in the United States of America
1-44844-35714-2/8/2018

Anger has Friday night dream duty, and Dream Productions is putting on a great show. Riley is a superhero battling a monster goalie with many arms.

"**BAM! POW! TAKE THAT!**" Anger yells. He bangs the control panel.

BUZZ! BUZZ! Riley's alarm clock goes off. She pounds the snooze button.

"It's Saturday," Riley grumbles. "I don't need to get up this early."

"Do you need a break?" Joy asks Anger. She yawns and rubs her eyes.

"I could take over if you want," Disgust adds.

Anger is too annoyed at all the little things going wrong this morning to pay attention to his friends. "First, that alarm clock wakes us up just as the dream was getting good. Now, get a load of that toothpaste! And that hair? It's really steaming me up!"

Riley walks downstairs for breakfast.

"Good morning, Sunshine," Riley's mom says. "Mrs. Das is coming over to help me with the garden. I told her that you could watch Devan while we work."

"But I wanted to hang out with Jada today," Riley complains. "I made cupcakes and everything."

"Can you meet Jada later?" Mom asks. "It'll only be a few hours."

"A few **HOURS**?" Riley groans. "Mom, I really don't want to."

"I need your help, Riley," Mom says. "I'd really appreciate it."

"Oh, all right," Riley sighs grumpily.

The doorbell rings, and Riley's mom rushes to answer it.

"Thank you so much for coming over, Kyra," she tells her friend.

"Any time," Kyra says. "Devan can't wait to play with Riley. Right, Devan?"

Devan doesn't say a word.

"Well, he looks like a lot of fun . . . **NOT**!" Anger groans.

"Aw, come on," Joy says. "It'll be fine. Riley's a great babysitter."

"I want to go home," Devan tells Riley after their moms head to the garden.

"What did I tell you guys?" Anger huffs.

"How about a fun board game?" Joy suggests. "That should help everyone feel better."

"Fine," Anger grumbles. "Let's give it a try."

Riley takes out a board game. She sees Devan looking at a photo of her when she was little. In the picture, she's jumping on a sofa cushion, pretending that she's surrounded by lava.

"That looks **FUN**!" Devan says. He climbs on the
cushion and starts jumping.

"Whoa! Devan, you might get hurt!" Riley says as she
helps Devan off the chair. "Let's play this game instead, okay?"

Devan starts to complain, but then he sees the box. "Okay.
I like this game!"

As Riley sets up the game, Devan grabs the dice. "I'm youngest, so I go first," he says.

"The rules say that we roll to see who goes first," Riley tells Devan.

"At home, the youngest goes first," Devan argues.

"Okay, but here, we play by the rules," Riley says.

"Then I'm not playing!" Devan pouts.

"**MY TURN**!" Anger yells. He tries to grab a control lever.

"Hold on, hold on," Joy says. "Let's think about this."

"Maybe Devan is sad," Sadness suggests. "Maybe he wants to be at home, thinking about the weight of life's problems."

"Maybe he's afraid of losing the game," Fear says. "It's making me anxious too!"

Riley takes a deep breath and puts the board game away.

"Do you want to play a different game?" she asks.

Devan shakes his head.

"How about playing outside?" Riley tries again.

"No," Devan says, still pouting.

"How's everything going in here?" Riley's mom asks, coming back inside.

"We're fine," Riley says quickly. Then she whispers to her mom, "I just need a minute alone. Is that okay?"

"Of course," her mom whispers back.

Riley leaves Devan with the moms and heads up to her bedroom. She tries to calm down, but the whole morning has been so frustrating! She picks up a pillow and screams into it.

"What are we going to do?" Fear worries. "This is a disaster!"

"Well, the screaming sure felt good!" Anger says.

"Look, Riley's starting to calm down," says Sadness. "I think this time-out is helping."

"We have to go back downstairs soon," Joy says. Then she gets an idea. "Hey! Maybe Devan's cranky because he's hungry. How about we get a **SNACK**?"

Disgust shrugs. "It's worth a shot."

Riley goes back downstairs when she's feeling calmer.

"Everything okay, sweetie?" Riley's mom whispers.

Riley nods. Then she asks, "Mrs. Das, do you think Devan is hungry? Can I get him a snack?"

"That would be wonderful, Riley," Mrs. Das answers. "Maybe a little fruit or some crackers. Thank you."

When the moms return to the garden, Riley takes Devan into the kitchen.

"Would you like some crackers?" she offers. Devan shakes his head.

"How about a banana?" she asks. Devan shakes his head again.

"Can I have one of those?" Devan asks. He points to the cupcakes on the counter.

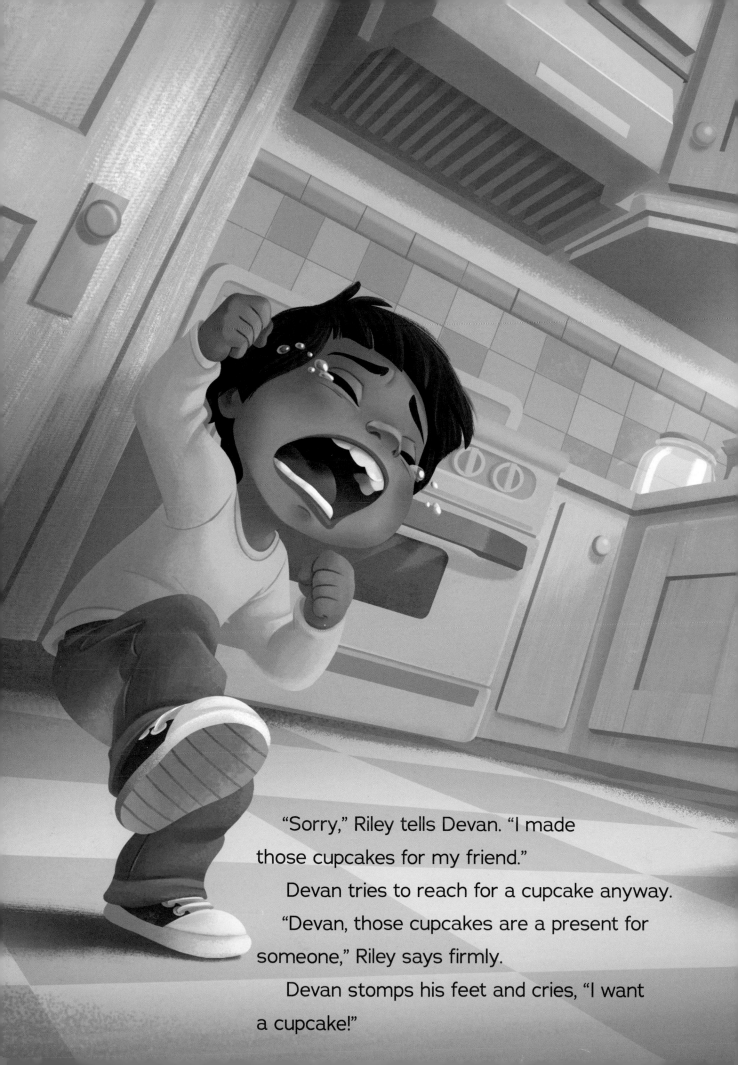

"Sorry," Riley tells Devan. "I made
those cupcakes for my friend."

Devan tries to reach for a cupcake anyway.

"Devan, those cupcakes are a present for
someone," Riley says firmly.

Devan stomps his feet and cries, "I want
a cupcake!"

"Step aside, Joy!" Anger steams. "This is our house, and these are our rules!"

"We need help!" Joy tells Sadness.

"Remember when Riley had tantrums?" Fear asks. "They were pretty scary."

"That's it!" Joy cries. "Guys, we need some tantrum memories—quick!"

"How about this one?" Sadness holds up a memory sphere. "When Riley first tried to ice-skate and couldn't stop falling? That was so sad."

"Sad?" Anger huffs. "That made me so mad!"

"Yes, you were definitely in control that day," Disgust says, shaking her head. "Screaming and crying and rolling around on the ground. Ugh."

"But Dad was great," Joy remembers. "He made Riley laugh when he sprinkled snow in her hair. He said, 'Sometimes hotheads need to learn how to **COOL DOWN**.'"

"Who's calling who a hothead?" Anger growls.

"Nobody's calling anyone anything," Joy answers.

Riley knows what it's like to feel angry and frustrated. She also knows how hard it can be to calm down. She wants to help Devan feel better. Suddenly, she has an idea.

"Devan, I'd like to tell you a story," she says. She begins to draw faces on her fingers. "Once upon a time, there was an angry little girl named Riley. She was having a really hard time learning to ice-skate."

"Every time she fell, she got angrier and angrier," Riley continues. "Until she just couldn't take it anymore."

"What did she do?" Devan sniffles.

"At first, she just yelled and cried," Riley says. "But that didn't help."

"What did help?" Devan asks.

"What helps you?" Fear asks Anger.

Anger thinks and says, "Well, I get cooler when Riley focuses on something fun."

"And the flames usually stop shooting out of your head when Riley takes deep breaths," Disgust adds.

"You usually share the console with me when Riley takes time to think or when she talks about how she feels," Sadness says.

Riley tells Devan the things that help her cool down.
"Can you tell me another story, Riley?" Devan asks.

"How about you tell me one?" Riley suggests. "We can make some puppets together."

"Cool!" Devan says with a big smile.

Riley and Devan make up funny stories to tell each other. They even decide to put on a puppet show for their moms!

"Phew!" Fear sighs. "That could have been a disaster!"

"Great **TEAMWORK**, everyone," Joy says, beaming.

Anger picks up a newspaper and smiles. "Gotta love that Riley. Puppets . . . just the best idea ever!"